DIEGO AND THE DINOSAURS

adapted by Lara Bergen
illustrated by Art Mawhinney

Ready-to-Read

Simon Spotlight/Nick Jr.
New York   London   Toronto   Sydney

Based on the TV series *Go, Diego, Go!*™ as seen on Nick Jr.®

SIMON SPOTLIGHT
An imprint of Simon & Schuster Children's Publishing Division
1230 Avenue of the Americas, New York, New York 10020
Manufactured in the United States of America
4 6 8 10 9 7 5 3
Library of Congress Cataloging-in-Publication Data
Bergen, Lara.
Diego and the dinosaurs / by Lara Bergen ; illustrated by Art Mawhinney. — 1st ed.
p. cm. — (Ready-to-read)
"Based on the TV series Go, Diego, Go!TM as seen on Nick Jr.®"—Copyright p.
ISBN-13: 978-1-4169-5825-3
ISBN-10: 1-4169-5825-8
1. Rebuses. I. Mawhinney, Art, ill. II. Go, Diego, go! (Television program) III. Title.
PZ7.B44985Die 2008
[E]—dc22
2007039997

Hi, I am  !
DIEGO
Look! I am back in the
time of the
DINOSAURS
for a rescue!

Do you like ?

DINOSAURS

So do we!

 lived a long, long time

DINOSAURS

ago.

Some  were big,

like this Brachiosaurus.

Some were small,

like this Microraptor.

This dinosaur is  .
MAIA

The **RAIN** washed away

her family's FOOTPRINTS.

Now  cannot find them. MAIA misses them a lot.

I know!
I will use my
to find them.

SPOTTING SCOPE

Do you see 's family

MAIA

in my  ?

SPOTTING SCOPE

Yes! There they are.

They are on  !

EGG   ISLAND

But wait!  is hungry.

MAIA

She is a plant eater.

She eats .

LEAVES

Do you see a TREE with lots of ? LEAVES
Yum!

Now we have to cross
the Rocky  cliffs.
ROCK
But look out!
There is a  slide!
ROCK

We need something soft to land on.

RESCUE PACK

can help us!

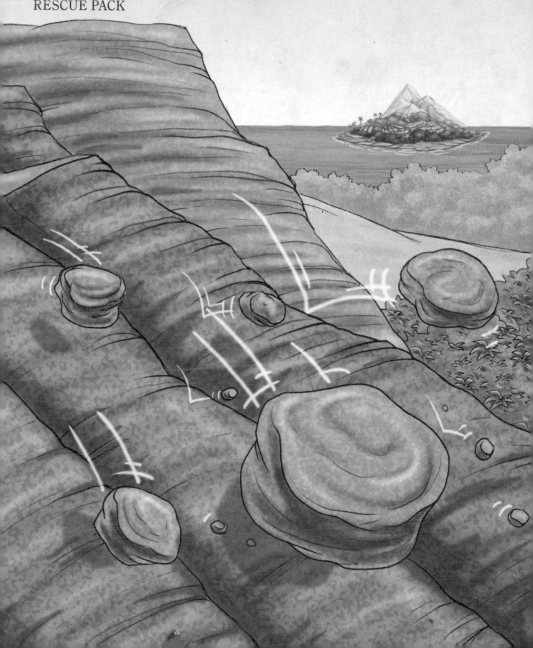

here!

Are soft to land on?

No!

Is a soft to land on?

No!

Is a big  soft to land on?
PILLOW

Yes!

Now we have to get
back up the  cliff.

ROCK

What can we climb?

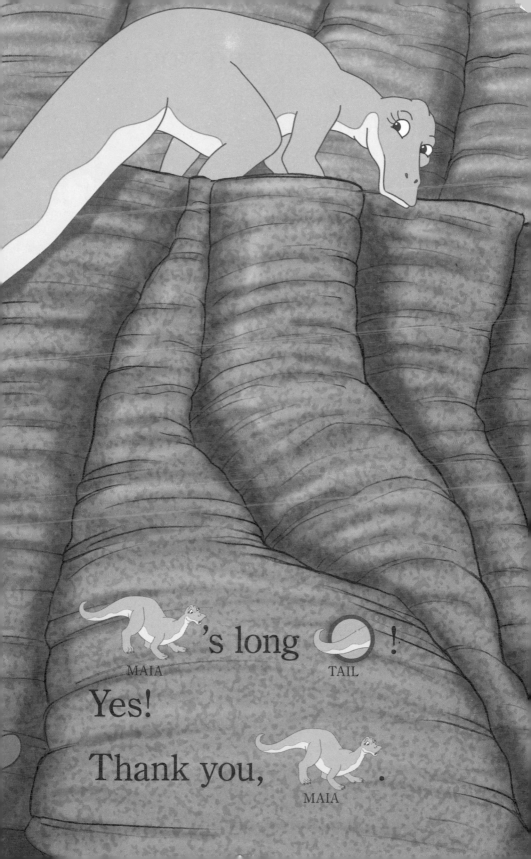

's long !

MAIA · TAIL

Yes!

Thank you, .

MAIA

Now we can find your family.

But wait!  smells another .

MAIA

DINOSAUR

 MAIA stomps her big FEET

to scare them away.

Will you stomp your FEET

like a  DINOSAUR too?

Yay! There they go!

Look! There is  EGG ISLAND !
But how will we get
across the WATER ?

Did you know that lots of
 could swim?
DINOSAURS

Can you swim
like a too?
DINOSAUR

Hooray! We made it to !

EGG   ISLAND

And look!

There is 's family!

MAIA

Do you see their
NEST

full of  ?
EGGS

We did it!

We helped  get home.

MAIA